LOLA LEVINE

LEVINE

IS NOT

Mean!

MONICA BROWN

LOLA LEVINE
IS NOT Mean!

ILLUSTRATED BY
Angela Dominguez

LITTLE, BROWN AND COMPANY
New York • Boston

Text copyright © 2015 by Monica Brown
Interior Artwork copyright © 2015 by Angela Dominguez
Text in excerpt from *Lola Levine: Drama Queen* copyright © 2016 by Monica Brown
Interior Artwork in excerpt from *Lola Levine: Drama Queen*
copyright © 2016 by Angela Dominguez
Soccer ball designed by Ruben Sheep—thenounproject.com

Little, Brown and Company

Hachette Book Group
1290 Avenue of the Americas, New York, NY 10104
Visit us at lb-kids.com

Little, Brown and Company is a division of Hachette Book Group, Inc.
The Little, Brown name and logo are trademarks of Hachette Book Group, Inc.

The publisher is not responsible for websites (or their content) that are not owned by the publisher.

First Paperback Edition: July 2016
First published in hardcover in November 2015 by Little, Brown and Company

The Library of Congress has cataloged the hardcover edition as follows:

Brown, Monica, 1969–
Lola Levine is not mean! / by Monica Brown. — First edition.
pages cm
Summary: Second-grader Lola has a wonderful family, a great teacher, and the best friend ever, Josh, and they all help her feel better after she is teased and forbidden to play team sports at recess for having accidentally hurt classmate Juan during a soccer game.
ISBN 978-0-316-25836-4 (hc) — ISBN 978-0-316-25838-8 (ebook)
[1. Teasing—Fiction.   2. Schools—Fiction.   3. Family life—Fiction.]   I. Title.
PZ7.B816644Lol 2015
[E]—dc23
2014041416

Paperback ISBN 978-0-316-25833-3

10

LSC-C

Printed in the United States of America

For Jeffrey, Bella, and Jules

CONTENTS

Dear *Diario*,

I'm getting really tired of being teased by the girls in my class. Everyone laughed at my new haircut yesterday, so I put on my favorite Peruvian hat—the one with the flaps around the ears—to cover it up. Then they laughed even harder! What they don't understand is that I cut my hair because it kept falling in my face and getting in the way during soccer games.

Mom says to *tell her* next time I want a haircut and she'll bring me to a beauty salon. But the last time I went to a beauty salon, I sneezed and sneezed. I think I'm allergic.

Shalom,
Lola Levine

1

Chapter One
Hello, Good-Bye, and Peace

My name is Lola Levine, and the truth is I'd rather *jump* on the bed than *go* to bed. Who wants to sleep when there are so many fun things to do? I'd much rather be reading or painting or writing in my diary or playing soccer. But my parents disagree. "Lights-out at eight," they say, because no matter what time I go to bed, I'm wide-awake by six AM. Even on weekends. My parents also think that six AM on Saturday morning is too early to juggle a soccer ball. (I certainly didn't *plan* to knock over my lamp and wake everyone up last Saturday!)

Sleep is overrated, in my opinion, and I have *lots* of opinions. For example, I think soccer is the greatest sport in the whole wide world. Every year on the first day of soccer practice, I wear a T-shirt that says MY GOAL IS STOPPING YOURS! I am a goalie. That's the position where you guard the goal and stop the forwards from scoring. In my opinion, forwards can be a little obnoxious, which is why I like to stop them.

My little brother, Ben, is a forward. A month ago, Ben slammed into a defender while trying to get to the ball. He ended up with two chipped teeth, which I thought looked cool. Mom and Dad didn't agree, though, so now he has to wear a mouth guard when he plays, which is a big black plastic thing that you wear to protect your teeth. Ben doesn't mind. In fact, he thinks his mouth guard makes him look fierce, so he wears it *all* the time. Except in class, that is, because it was grossing everyone out when he talked.

Thwump! Ben is bouncing his soccer ball against my door. Again.

"Hey, Lola!" he yells from the other side. "Wanna hear a joke?"

"No," I say, knowing that won't stop him.

Thwump! I hear again. "What do you call a pig who plays soccer?" Ben asks.

"A ball hog," I say, rolling my eyes, even though Ben can't see me through the door.

"Duh," Ben says. "That was an easy one. How about this: Why are soccer players so smart?"

I open the door, which isn't such a good idea, since Ben is there with his soccer ball. He heads the ball over my shoulder before I have a chance to react.

"Goooooooooooooal!" he yells. "Soccer players are smart because we use our heads!" And he's off and running down the hall, screaming, "I scored on Lola! I scored on Lola!"

"Ben," I say, "Mom said no more doorway soccer!"

Doorway soccer is a game Ben and I made up one day when it was raining outside and we were bored. The hallway was the field, and the doors to our bedrooms were the goals. But after Ben fell down the stairs trying to get to the ball, Mom and Dad said, "No more!" and drove us to the rec center.

The thing you need to know about Ben is that he has what our parents call "a strong personality." They also say he takes after me. He's okay as far as little brothers go, except when he sticks out his tongue at me behind Mom's back, which he hardly ever does now that he's wearing a mouth guard. Or when he goes into my room without permission. I hate that. Well, I'll just say I dislike it very much, because as Mom says, "hate" is a strong word and she'd rather I didn't use it. Mom is a writer for the newspaper, so she has lots of opinions about words. Especially mine.

Like Mom, I'm a writer. I don't write for a newspaper (yet), but I write in my diary, I write letters, and I write notes to everyone in my family, especially when I'm upset. Sometimes I leave these notes in surprising places, like the dishwasher or inside Ben's shoe. Sometimes I write what I call "convincing" notes. These are notes I use when I'm trying to get my family to do something. It's better than being a pest, according to Mom. For example, on my nightstand, there is a frame. In the frame, there is a note. The note says:

Dear Mom and Dad,

This is where I will put a picture of my kitty. If I ever get a kitty.

Shalom,
Lola Levine

I like the word "shalom" because it means three things: "hello," "good-bye," and "peace." My dad taught it to me. My dad is Jewish. My mom is Catholic. A boy at school said I was a half-and-half once. I disliked that very much. Mom and Dad tell me that I'm whole just the way I am, and I agree.

My note is a little hint for Mom and Dad, because I really want a kitty. Each day, I try to convince Mom and Dad a little more. But Mom says that birthdays are one day a year and cats are forever. I love animals—all animals, big or small, with claws or paws or scales. But so far the only pet I have is Mia, my goldfish. I named her after Mia Hamm, who was only fifteen when she joined the US Women's National Soccer Team. She won two Olympic gold medals and two World Cups. I love my pet, but as I keep telling Mom, you can't cuddle a fish. I've been dropping big and little hints about a kitty for a few months now.

I think having a kitty might make me feel better about not having too many friends at school. I do have one super best friend, though. His name is Josh Blot, and we do lots of stuff together. When Josh is sick and doesn't come to school, it's a big bummer because I'm pretty much on my own. No one else picks me for a partner or to play with at recess. Especially not Alyssa Goldstein or Makayla Miller, the most popular girls in my class at Northland Elementary School. Alyssa and Makayla are best friends, of course.

"You do realize that a girl can't have a best friend that's a *boy*, right?" Makayla told me just last week. She and Alyssa are *always* bugging me about something. They make fun of my hair, my clothes, what I say, and what I do. I get pretty tired of it, actually.

"Why can't a girl be best friends with a boy?" I asked, but I didn't have time to hear her answer because just then Josh ran up.

"Race you to the fence, Lola!" he said, and we were off. We tied, but Josh got a splinter because his hand hit the fence so hard. I helped him pull it out because that's what best friends are for, right?

Chapter Two
The Orange Smoothies

On Monday morning, I wake up, cross my fingers, touch the picture of Briana Scurry on my wall, and turn around three times for luck. Briana Scurry was the goalie for the US Olympic women's soccer team when they won gold medals in 1996 and 2004. She is, in my opinion, the best goalie that has ever played the game. I got the photo last year for my seventh birthday, along with an Olympic soccer jersey, which is my very favorite shirt, even though it's white, which is a boring color, in my opinion. My *favorite* color is purple, which is why Dad and I painted the walls of my room purple last summer.

We also painted orange polka dots for my soccer team, the Orange Smoothies. We are number one in our league. I wanted us to be called the Orange Fireballs or the Orange Tigers, but Alyssa suggested the Orange Smoothies and everyone liked that name better. Alyssa is my least favorite member of the Orange Smoothies. She is, in my opinion, a show-off. She is also a forward.

Today I'm feeling a little bit red, so I run down the stairs, out the door, and across the yard into my dad's art studio, where he's already working on a great big colorful painting.

"Dad! Can I borrow some red paint?" I ask.

"Of course," he says, "but don't be late for breakfast."

He and I mix up a really cool red color, and ten minutes later, my bedroom closet has bright red flowers floating over the grass that Josh and I painted last weekend. Josh thinks it's cool that I can paint on my closet whenever I want. I tell him it's just because my dad is an artist who

believes in "creative expression." Josh's mom is the principal of our school, and she doesn't let Josh paint on the walls.

I open my window to help the paint dry, then get dressed for school, take our stairs two at a time, and karate-kick the door into the kitchen open.

Ben is already at the table.

"*Dolores,*" he says, "I scored on you!" Lola is short for Dolores, which means "pain" in Spanish, and Ben knows that I don't like my full name, even if I'm named after my *tía* Lola and even if she's the most awesome aunt ever. Tía Lola uses a nickname, and I do, too. I just wish my *tía* Lola didn't live so far away—she's all the way in Peru, a whole different continent! My middle name is Esther, and sometimes my *bubbe,* my grandma Levine, calls me that because it was *her* grandma's name. Unfortunately, my *bubbe* lives far away, too.

"Mind your own business, *Benjamin*," I say, but it doesn't have the same effect. As I spread cream cheese on my bagel, Ben just sticks out his tongue and starts tapping out a rhythm with his spoon. He does this to annoy me.

Mom is wearing her red suit when she pokes into the kitchen and says, "*Buenos días*, Lola! Good morning, Benito!" She comes over and kisses us each on the head. "Lola, don't forget your lunch today," she says, wrapping her arms around me in a big hug. Sometimes I accidentally forget my lunch, especially when Dad accidentally puts cauliflower in it. Cauliflower is a white food that I dislike very much.

"Ben," Mom says, "wash your face and brush your hair!"

"*Dolores,*" Ben says, "can you help?"

Ben's hair is long and curly and crazy and sticking up—as usual.

"Fine," I say. "But DON'T call me Dolores!"

"Okay, Dol—I mean Lola," Ben says. Ben hates getting his hair cut, and a year ago, on his fifth birthday, he announced that he wouldn't get it cut anymore. Ever. Dad thought this was a form of creative expression, so he agreed to it.

"*For now,*" Mom said. "And only if he can keep the knots out." Since Dad has a ponytail himself, I think he was secretly glad.

Ben and I manage to get all his hair under control.

Mom pours herself a cup of *café con leche*, and I ask if she has a big interview for the paper.

"How'd you know?" Mom asks with a wink.

"Because you're wearing your red suit,"

I say, "which matches the flowers I just painted on my closet."

"I know," says Mom.

"How'd you know?" I ask, dipping my bagel into Mom's sweet, milky coffee. Mom just smiles, picks up her napkin, and wipes a spot of red paint from my nose.

Chapter Three
Five-Minute Warning Bell

Mom drops us off at Northland Elementary School on her way to work. I walk Ben into his kindergarten classroom at the front of the building, and then I go down the long hall to Ms. Garcia's second-grade classroom all by myself.

"*Hola,* Lola!" Ms. Garcia says with a smile when I walk through the door.

"*Buenos días,* Ms. Garcia. *¿Cómo estás?*" I say, smiling back.

"*Muy bien, gracias,* Lola," Ms. Garcia says. Ms. Garcia knows that I like to practice my Spanish as often as I can. When I finally get to visit my *tía* Lola in Peru, I want to show her how much I've learned.

Ms. Garcia is a great teacher, in my opinion. She is one of my favorite people in the whole wide world. On the very first day of second grade, Ms. Garcia took roll. She called out, "Levine, Dolores." My name sounded pretty the way she said it, rolling the *r* just like my mom does, but that didn't stop Alyssa from snorting behind me. I raised my hand to tell Ms.

Garcia my nickname, but she was already on to Lopez, Olivia, and Miller, Makayla. So before I went home for the day, I left a note wrapped around Ms. Garcia's purple pen.

Dear Ms. Garcia,

Please call me Lola. I don't like the name Dolores and I don't want to be teased by Alyssa. Last year she made up a rhyme. "Dolores is a pain, just like her name!"

I ~~hated~~ disliked that very much.

Shalom,
Lola Levine

Ms. Garcia started calling me Lola the very next day.

Today Josh meets me at my desk.

"Hey, Lola!" he says. "What's up?!"

"Not much," I say. "How's Milo?" Josh may not be allowed to paint on the walls, but he does have a big cute cuddly cat.

"He coughed up the biggest hair ball ever this weekend!" Josh says, and we both laugh.

I can tell it's going to be a great day.

On Monday afternoons, we get an extra-long recess, and we usually play soccer.

"Boys against girls!" I yell, grabbing the ball and running outside.

"Why don't we have a mixed team for once?" Alyssa whines.

"Yeah, Lola," says Makayla with her hands on her hips.

"That would definitely be more fair… to the girls," Juan says, laughing, which really annoys me.

"Juan Gomez," I say in my loudest voice, "you boys only won by two points last Monday, so stop bragging!"

"You're not in charge, Lola," Alyssa says, and goes over to stand by Juan. Alyssa like-likes Juan, but that doesn't mean she has to agree with everything he says, does it?

"Let's just play," Josh jumps in. "Boys against girls this week, then mixed teams next week." No one wants to argue with

Josh, not even Alyssa, because Josh is nice, cute, popular, and Principal Blot's son. Not that I think Josh is cute or anything, but I know other girls do. Last year, Olivia Lopez gave Josh a great big red lollipop on Valentine's Day with a note that said "Won't you be mine?" Josh turned as red as the lollipop and didn't even say thank you. After school, he and I cracked it into pieces and ate it with our fingers. It was yummy.

Josh walks toward the soccer field, and we follow.

"On your toes, everyone!" I say. "Let's be tough!"

"You know, Lola, some of us actually *like* boys," Alyssa says.

"I like boys," I say, and I really do. "I like beating them at soccer."

"Someday, when you're older, you'll understand," Makayla says, rolling her eyes.

"I'm two months older than you, Makayla!" I say, not noticing that the game has started until Juan takes a shot that whizzes past me.

"Goooooooooooooooooal," Juan says, flapping his arms. Ugh.

We play hard, and soon we are tied up, 1–1. We hear the five-minute warning bell, and I know that this is our chance to take the lead.

"Come on, girls!" I say. "Step up!" Juan drives past the midfielders, and he's headed straight toward our goal. I can't let him score again. He's fast, but so am I. I come out of my box and decide to go for a slide tackle—I leave my feet and slide sideways toward him, hoping my foot will reach the ball in time. Instead of hitting the ball, though, my feet hit Juan's ankle, and he falls. Hard. He doesn't get up.

"Foul!" the boys yell.

"What's wrong with you, Lola?!" Alyssa says, and runs over to Juan.

"I'm so sorry," I tell Juan, but he just says, "Go away, Lola!" He's grabbing his ankle, and I can tell he's trying really hard not to cry.

"You are so mean, Lola!" says Makayla. "Can't you play sports like a normal person?"

I want to ask Makayla how a normal person plays sports, but I don't get a chance because just then I look up to see Principal Blot marching toward us.

"Uh-oh," says Josh.

"*Double* uh-oh," I say back.

Principal Blot takes one look at Juan and asks Josh to go get the nurse. Everyone starts talking at once, and the next thing I know, I'm in Principal Blot's office.

Did I say this was going to be a great day? Boy, was I ever wrong.

Chapter Four
Mean Lola Levine

The next day at recess, I sit on the bench all by myself. Principal Blot won't let me play team sports until I've learned my lesson, which means no tag, no kickball, and worst of all, no soccer. Josh is the only one who walks over to say hello.

"Well, at least my mom didn't call your parents," Josh says. "Want to meet at the park after school?"

"No, thanks," I say, looking down. "I've got too much homework." Which isn't actually true. I know it's not Josh's fault, but I just don't want to be with anyone whose last name is Blot.

"Okay, Lola, whatever you say," Josh says with a frown, and leaves me alone.

Watching him walk off, I'm already sorry I said I wouldn't meet him. Recess by myself lasts a long time, so I decide to write Josh a note.

Dear Josh,

Sorry I said I couldn't go to the park. I'm just grumpy. I think it's because I'm trying to learn my lesson. See you tomorrow.

Shalom,
Lola Levine

My disaster day turns into a disaster week. Juan is limping, and everyone is mad at me. No one (but Josh) is speaking to me. Not only am I not allowed to play sports at recess, but I have a new nickname at school. Everyone is calling me Mean Lola Levine. Alyssa started it. I dislike it very much.

I write Juan a note and sneak it into his lunch box.

Dear Juan,

I'm sorry I used a slide tackle on you
at recess, and I'm sorry I made you
cry. You are a good soccer player.

Shalom,
Lola Levine

Juan writes me back right away:

Dear Mean Lola Levine,

You didn't make me cry. I had
something in my eye. And that
wasn't a slide tackle. That was
a foul.

Juan

The next few days are pretty lonely. I sit on the bench and walk around the playground by myself most of the time. Josh comes and walks with me a little every day, but not for long. Someone always comes and invites him to be captain of the kickball team, or runs up and tags him and says, "You're it!" like Alyssa did today. At least no one calls me Mean Lola Levine in Ms. Garcia's class. They wouldn't dare.

During class, Ms. Garcia tells us we will have a big surprise during science next week.

"Can you give us a hint?" asks Makayla.

"Well…," says Ms. Garcia, "I can tell you that it's a *wriggly* surprise."

"Are we getting a class kitty?" I ask hopefully, but Ms. Garcia just shakes her head and laughs.

"No, Lola, not a kitten, but something really cool and special. I'll give you all one more hint. The surprise has to do with garbage." Some kids groan, because they don't think garbage is very exciting, but not me. Other than art, science is my favorite subject, and I know that if Ms. Garcia says that garbage is exciting, it will be. Besides, with everyone mad at me, I need something to look forward to. I leave a sticky note on Josh's pencil case.

Dear Josh,

Soccer? After school? Today?

Shalom,
Lola Levine

At recess, Josh comes up to me and says, "I can't play after school today because we have to take Milo to the vet. He has a runny nose."

"That's awful!" I say. I love Josh's cat, Milo, though I don't get to see him very often. Josh's mom hardly ever lets him have friends over. Maybe she gets tired of seeing kids all day because she's the principal.

As the week goes by, I notice things are a little weird at home. At first, I can't figure out what it is, but then I realize. It's quiet! Ben is too quiet. There aren't any *thwump*s or "Doloreses" or even any soccer jokes. Ben doesn't even comment when I wear my Peruvian hat, the one he says makes me look like a dog, with the flaps around the ears.

"Can you make my hair look cool?" Ben asks at breakfast on Thursday. He hands me Mom's hair spray. Now I *know* something is wrong.

"Ben," I ask, "since when do you want cool hair?"

"Can you keep a secret?" asks Ben.

"Depends on the secret," I say.

"I like a girl."

"Really?" I say, and try not to laugh, since it seems like Ben is pretty serious. "Who?"

"Her name is Mira."

"Mira who?" I ask.

"Mira Goldstein," he says. "Her sister's in your class."

Ugh. My brother likes Alyssa Goldstein's little sister. I didn't even know she had a little sister.

"She's the coolest girl in the whole class," Ben says.

I try not to laugh.

"Um, Ben," I ask, "what do you mean by 'like'?"

"It means I want to share paints with her in art and for us to choose each other for teams," Ben says.

"And do you and Mira share paints in art and choose each other for teams?" I ask.

"Well, I'm so good at sports, everyone chooses me for teams," he says with a smile. That's my brother! But then he frowns.

"But ever since my mouth guard fell into the blue paint, no one wants to share paints with me."

"Oh, I see," I say, and I do. Poor Ben. I do my best to flatten his wild, curly hair. It's not really working, and I'm starting to choke on the hair spray.

"All done," I say.

"Thanks, *Dolores*," Ben says, and I know he's feeling a little better.

"Want to help me make a quick get-well card for Josh's cat?" I ask.

"Sure!" he says, and we get to work. I write and Ben draws.

Dear Milo,

You are so cute and fluffy.
We are sorry your nose is stuffy!

Get better, okay?

Shalom,
Lola Levine +
Ben Levine

"I'm going to tape this to Josh's back-pack!" says Ben.

"Great idea," I agree.

Chapter Five
Pencil Power

On Friday, I'm *still* Mean Lola Levine. I'm so glad when the final bell rings and it's the weekend and I can just be with my family. I need a break from school. At least Ben's in a better mood, I think, as he runs up to me with a big smile.

"Guess what, Lola?" Ben asks.

"Mira shared paints with you today?" I ask.

"No, something even better. It's my turn to bring George home this weekend!" George is Ben's class pet—a furry, cuddly guinea pig.

"Don't tell Mira you like George better than her," I say, laughing.

Ben grabs my hand. "Dad's loading George into the car right now. Let's go!" It's hard to miss Dad across the parking lot loading a guinea pig into his orange car, what he calls his people mover.

"Hello, favorite humans!" Dad says as we climb into the car. I lean sideways and look into George's cage, but he's hiding in his little house and I can't see him.

"I'll help you take care of George," I tell Ben. "I'm great with animals."

"No way, *Dolores!*" says Ben. "He's my class pet. He's sleeping in my room, and I'm in charge!"

"Okay, okay," I say, "but be careful. This is our chance to show Mom and Dad that we can handle a pet! A furry one."

Ben snorts and puts in his mouth guard, so that's the end of *that* conversation.

Friday night dinner at our house is always fun. My mom and my dad are both good cooks, and they always make something special to welcome the weekend. Tonight we have matzo ball soup, Peruvian chicken, and flan, three of my favorite things to eat. I almost forget about my bad week.

"How are things at school, Lola?" Mom asks. I don't really want to answer her, but I do anyway.

"Not that great. I'm not having any fun at recess," I say.

"But you love recess, Lola! It's your chance to run around and play soccer," Mom says.

"Well, I haven't exactly been running around lately. I have been walking, though. Sometimes I walk with Josh, and sometimes I walk around all by myself."

"What about your other friends?" Mom asks. I explain to her and Dad that Alyssa and her group don't like me.

"But that's only a few people," Dad says. "What about the rest of the children in your class?" Finally I have to tell them.

"Well, the other kids play tag, or soccer, or kickball, which is fun, but Principal

Blot told me that I am not allowed to play group sports at recess anymore because I'm too competitive."

"You are competitive, and there's nothing wrong with that! Why does Ms. Blot think you are *too* competitive?" Mom asks.

"Well," I say, "on Monday, I slide tackled Juan Gomez a little too hard, and he fell and hurt his ankle."

"I know you would never hurt anyone on purpose, Lola, and accidents happen," my mom says.

"I'm not sure slide tackling is a good idea at school, though," Dad adds.

"I know it isn't," I say. It's weird. Once I tell Mom and Dad about Principal Blot and Juan, I feel better, so I keep going. I tell them about Alyssa making fun of my hair and name and about everyone calling me Mean Lola Levine. I even tell them what Makayla said—that a girl can't have a best friend that's a boy.

"That's ridiculous!" Dad says.

"I'm going to have a talk with Ms. Blot on Monday," Mom says with a frown. I feel sorry for Ms. Blot already. But then I think about it.

"Mom, let me try writing Principal Blot a letter before you talk to her."

"Okay, my little writer," Mom says with a smile.

"Pencil power," I say, and Mom and I fist-bump.

"Group hug!" says my goofy dad, and he and Mom hold me tight. Even Ben joins in.

"Just remember, Lola," Mom says, "no one has the right to treat you badly."

"That's right," says Dad, and finally I feel all the way better.

"Hey," I say with only a little sniffle, "how about a game of tag?"

"Yes!" says Ben, and Mom and Dad agree, so after dinner we go out into the backyard. It's Mom and me against Dad and Ben. Guess who wins? We do, of course, but only because it's so easy to tag Dad with his long ponytail flying out behind him.

On Saturday morning, I knock on Ben's door. I really want to pet George the guinea pig. "What's the password?" Ben asks. Hmmm, I can't remember. It used to be "Bend it like Beckham," after David Beckham, a soccer player with a great kick, but he changed it.

"Give me a hint," I say.

"Okay," Ben says, "think Brazil."

Well, that's easy.

"Pelé," I say.

"Pelé what?" Ben asks.

"Pelé *el rey!*" I yell, which means "Pelé the king!" Pelé was a Brazilian soccer player who was the best the world had ever seen. Ben got a picture book called

Pelé, King of Soccer when he was four, and he has loved Pelé ever since. The book is worn and the pages are torn, but when Ben is sad or tired, he still reads it.

"Come in," Ben says. He's sitting criss-cross applesauce with George the guinea pig in his lap. He's feeding him a carrot. I pet George, and he chirps like a little bird.

All of a sudden, Ben's eyes bug out.

"Something's happening!" he yells.

"George is chirping," I say calmly. "That's what guinea pigs do."

"No, no!" Ben says, and he practically throws George off his lap.

"Be careful!" I say as George scurries under the bed. At least that's where I think he goes. I'm looking at Ben. I see the problem. George has pooped on Ben's leg. Ben is starting to gag. He has what Dad calls a weak stomach, which just means he throws up easily, like in cars, on airplanes, and once on a ride at the fair.

"Mom!" I yell. "Dad!" I am afraid that Ben is going to throw up. "It's just a little poop. Everyone poops," I say to Ben, thinking of a book I once read. I don't understand my brother—he wears a gross mouth guard every day, but a little guinea pig poop makes him sick? I grab some tissues and clean Ben up. Then I grab a washcloth and clean him up some more, which is what I'm doing when Mom and Dad finally make it to the crisis. They figure things out right away.

"Come on, buddy," Dad says, "let's go outside." He picks up Ben and heads to the backyard. I'm glad, because if Ben is going to throw up, I sure don't want to see it.

"Lola," Mom says, "I have a question for you.... WHERE is George?!"

"Well, Ben sort of threw him under the bed." I crawl under the bed to look, but there is no George. I do see some LEGOs and my old shin guard—so that's where it went! "No guinea pig in here," I say, and Mom gets on her knees to start looking, too.

"Let me think," I say to Mom. "If I were George the guinea pig, where would I go? Guinea pigs like to burrow, so...the closet!" Ben's closet is a scary place. It is a mixture of dirty clothes, shoes, and old worn-out stuffed animals that he doesn't let Mom throw away. About once a month,

Dad makes Ben clean out his closet, but judging by the mess, I think Dad's slipping. Sure enough, there's George the guinea pig in the corner under a pile of dirty soccer socks.

"I found him!" I yell to Mom, who claps.

"Good job, Lola!" she says, but I'm not quick enough, and George runs between my legs and into the hall. Next thing I know, George is in my room and under my bed.

"Wait," I say, thinking of doorway soccer. "Let me get my keeper gloves on. Can you bring me a carrot?" I ask Mom.

"Smart thinking," she says, and a few seconds later, she's back with the carrot. I put it near the door and wait.

"He's got to get hungry sometime," I

say. When George comes out, I'm ready. I catch him and don't let go until he's safe in his cage. Mom and I let him keep the carrot.

"Yeah!" says Mom.

"Teamwork!" I say, and we do a little victory dance. It's almost like saving a goal.

Chapter Six

Meow! *¡Miau!*

On Monday morning, I go to Principal Blot's office with my note. She's at her desk sipping a cup of coffee and looking at something on her computer.

"Hello, Lola," she says. "How can I help you?"

"I wrote you a letter," I say, and start to hand it to her.

"Since you are here, why don't you just read it to me?" she says.

Talking is harder than writing, but I do what Ms. Blot asks.

Dear Principal Blot,

I wish I didn't hurt Juan Gomez while playing soccer. It was an accident, and I said sorry to Juan. But people get hurt playing sports, and it isn't always someone's fault. If you let me play at recess, I will try to be much more careful, because I know I am very strong and competitive.

Shalom,
Lola Levine

When I'm finished, Principal Blot looks at me and says, "That was a very well-written note, Lola. You may resume playing sports at recess."

"Thank you, Principal Blot," I say with a smile. Principal Blot *almost* smiles back. I get to play tag and soccer and kickball again! Of course, it would be more fun if everyone weren't still mad at me, but I know Josh will pick me for his team.

He does, and at recess, I get to play soccer! Alyssa and Makayla are on the opposite team. Every time they dribble near the goal, they yell things like "Watch out for Mean Lola Levine" or "Don't foul me, *Dolores*." I try not to let it bother me, but I guess it bothers Josh.

"Lola Levine is NOT mean!" Josh

says, picking up the soccer ball and stopping the game. "She's just a good soccer player."

"Oh, yeah?" says Alyssa. "Well, I think she is mean. I think she's mean, mean, MEAN Lola Levine!"

"She's not!" Josh says. "In fact, Lola Levine is a..."

"Lola Levine is a...what?" Alyssa says with her hands on her hips.

"Lola Levine is a...soccer queen!" Josh yells, and for a minute no one says anything. Josh's face is turning redder by the second. I'm so happy, I want to hug him, which is weird because even though Josh is my best friend, I've never wanted to hug him before. I remind myself never to ask him to share paints.

Alyssa starts to say something else, but all of a sudden, Juan Gomez steps in front of her.

"Lola IS a pretty awesome soccer player," Juan says. "Can we stop talking and just play?"

We do. My team loses, and for the first time ever, I don't even mind. After the game, I walk over to Juan.

"I really am sorry about the slide tackle, and you were right, it was a foul," I say.

"That's okay," Juan says, smiling, "but from now on let's try to be on the same team... *soccer queen*."

That night I write a note to my mom and leave it wrapped around her toothbrush.

Dear Mom,

My note worked! I played soccer at
recess today, and things are much
better. My friends are still mostly
boys, but that's just fine with me.

Shalom,
Lola Levine,
Soccer Queen

P.S. You are the best mom in the
whole wide world.
P.P.S. Meow! Meow!

When I wake up, I have a note taped
to the wall by my bed. Mom's so sneaky.
Here's what it says:

My sweet Lola Levine,

Being your mom makes me happy every day.

Te quiero mucho,
Mom

P.S. *¡Miau! ¡Miau!*

What? *¡Miau!* Did my mom just meow me back in Spanish? Could this mean I might actually get a kitty? I smile big. Today I don't cross my fingers, touch Briana Scurry's picture, or turn around for luck. I just don't think I'll need it. I can't wait for school. Today we find out about Ms. Garcia's science surprise!

But first I run down the hall to Mom and Dad's room. Mom is still getting ready for work.

"I got your note, Mom!" I say, and give her a giant hug. "Meow?" I ask.

"Well," Mom says, "we wanted to surprise you, but you know I can't keep a happy secret. Your dad and I think you have shown us enough responsibility to have a pet—a furry one, that is...."

"Thank you! *iGracias!*" I say, jumping up and down.

"We thought this summer might be a good time to go to the Humane Society and pick out a kitty. *¿Bueno?*" Mom asks.

"Super *bueno!*" I say, and run down the hall to tell Ben.

Chapter Seven
Wriggly Science

"Boys and girls," Ms. Garcia says after lunch, "it's time to talk about our new science project."

Finally! I am very excited. At the front of the classroom are shallow plastic containers, a pile of shredded newspapers, a bag of sand, and a big red mystery bucket. There is also a bunch of what can only be described as garbage. There is a box of orange peels and eggshells and what looks like carrots and maybe some coffee grounds. There are also *lots* of extra chairs in our classroom.

"The first part of this surprise is that we will be partnering with the kindergartners for this project," Ms. Garcia says. "They will be your little buddies, and I expect that all of you second graders will show them what it means to listen, follow directions, raise your hand when you want to speak, and most importantly, respect others. Can you do this?"

"Yes!" we say together, and just then there's a knock at the door. Ms. Garcia

opens the door, and a parade of kindergartners walks in.

I see my brother right away. He looks
little and nervous and immediately comes
over to sit by me. I try not to laugh at his
slicked-back hair.

"Which one is Mira?" I whisper to
him. He points to the girl sitting next to
Alyssa. Mira has bright red hair and is
even smaller than Ben. She's holding
Alyssa's hand and looks scared. I smile.

"How's the paint sharing going, Ben?"
I ask.

"Pretty good," he says with a mouth-
guard-free smile.

"Attention, please," Ms. Garcia says in a
voice that gets everyone's attention. "Today
we are going to learn how to turn garbage

into soil for our school garden using nature's best recyclers!" Then Ms. Garcia reaches into the red bucket and pulls out a handful of squirmy, gooey red worms.

"These are called red wigglers, and they are going to help us compost!" Ms. Garcia says. All of a sudden, I hear a big gulp. I look at Ben. He seems a little pale. Uh-oh.

"All we need," Ms. Garcia goes on, "is shredded newspapers, sand, a little water, the fruit and vegetable leftovers from your lunch boxes, and our worm friends, and we have something we call vermicomposting. Can you say 'vermicomposting'?"

"Vermicomposting," the class repeats.

"How does it work?" Juan asks.

"Well, the worms eat the garbage, and their poop turns into nutritious fertilizer that we'll use in our class garden," Ms.

Garcia says. Ben grabs my hand, and I get worried.

"Worm poop...," he whispers. I can tell he's trying not to look up at Ms. Garcia's red wigglers.

"Are you okay?" I ask. He shakes his head. He is definitely *not* okay. I'm trying to decide what to do as Ms. Garcia goes on with her explanation.

"We leave this pan under the plastic container, which has holes in it to capture the liquid that drips through the compost.... We call this liquid worm tea, and it's a great plant food. It also scares away other insects."

"Worm tea?" Ben says, and that's it. He starts gagging. I raise my hand, but I'm already pulling Ben out of the classroom and out the door so he can have some fresh air.

"He's going to be sick!" I tell Ms. Garcia. We make it outside, but I know it's too late. I'm just lucky we make it to the garbage can. Poor Ben. I try to be like Mom and pat his back. Ms. Garcia walks toward us, and it looks like half the class is staring out the window. Great.

"He has a weak stomach," I tell her. "He'll be okay."

"Still, why don't you take him to the nurse to be sure," says Ms. Garcia, and she heads back to the classroom.

I take him to the drinking fountain to rinse his mouth first, and suddenly, there's a little red-haired girl beside us. It's Mira.

"Ben, are you okay?" Mira asks. Ben is red with embarrassment, but then Mira takes his hand. He smiles, and I think he forgets he just threw up in front of forty kids.

"Ms. Garcia says I can walk with Ben to the nurse's office," Mira tells me.

"Thanks, Mira." I smile, and the three of us go see Nurse Mary.

I'm pretty sure Ben will be fine now that he's not in sight of the worms. Nurse

Mary decides that Ben won't go back to the classroom until science class is over. She takes him to the library, and Mira and I walk back to the classroom together.

I take Mira over to Alyssa and say, "You know, Alyssa, you have an awesome sister."

"I know," Alyssa says, and she actually smiles at me, maybe for the first time ever. I decide that any girl with a little sister as cool as Mira can't be all bad, so I smile back.

"Want to help us bury worms in garbage?" Alyssa asks, and I say okay. But when I start talking to the red wigglers, Alyssa rolls her eyes and snorts.

I'm in such a good mood, it doesn't bother me one bit.

Chapter Eight
Hello, Good-Bye, and Peace

My name is Lola Levine, and the truth is I'd rather *jump* on the bed than *go* to bed. Who wants to sleep when there are so many fun things to do? I'd much rather be reading or painting or writing in my diary or playing soccer, or even burying worms in garbage with my worst enemy. Of course, Mom doesn't like the word "enemy." She'd prefer I didn't use it. After everything that has happened in second grade so far, I can see why.

I can't sleep. I'm meeting Josh in the park after school tomorrow to play soccer, because he's my super best friend and he doesn't care if I play like a normal person or not. I'm trying to think of a new nickname for him—something as cool as Lola Levine, Soccer Queen. But I can't think of anything. Josh Blot, Polka Dot? Josh Blot, Pepper Pot? Laughs a Lot? Tip-top? Maybe not.

Oh, well. I'll just go to sleep. But first I write a quick note in my diary.

Dear *Diario*,

Things are pretty great. We are going
to get a kitty this summer, and I
can hardly wait. I wonder if kitties
like soccer. I sure do. The Orange
Smoothies' spring season starts next
week. Of course, I'll wear my T-shirt
that says MY GOAL IS STOPPING YOURS!
I can't wait!

    Most importantly, though, I have a
super best friend who I like very much
and the most awesome family in the
whole wide world.

                  Shalom,
                  Lola Levine,
                  Soccer Queen

P.S. Meow! *¡Miau!*

Don't miss
Lola's next adventure!

Available now

Dear *Diario*,

I can't sleep. I want to juggle my soccer
ball, but I'm pretty sure that would
wake everyone else up. I could paint
on the walls of my room, but I'm not
feeling full of what my artist dad calls
"creative expression." What I am feeling
full of is energy—inside and out.

Sometimes my thoughts are like
monkeys jumping up and down in
my head saying, "Ooh-ooh, aah-aah!"
Sometimes my monkeys are swinging
from trees.

I'm excited for school tomorrow
because Ms. Garcia says there will
be a surprise. I *love* surprises. I can't
imagine anything better than the last

surprise, which involved worms and garbage.

My monkeys are getting tired.

Shalom and *buenas noches*,
Lola Levine

Chapter One
Walk, Don't Run

My name is Lola Levine, and the truth is little brothers are sometimes a pain. At least mine is.

"Lola! Zola! Granola! It's time to get up!" yells Ben right in my ear.

"Ouch," I say, and pull the covers over my head. Usually I am up way before Ben. Why am I so tired? Oh yeah—I couldn't sleep.

"Cow barn," I mumble into my pillow. I can't say "darn" because that's a word Mom would rather I didn't use.

"It just doesn't sound nice," she says.

"Dolores! Boris! Morris! Wake up!" Ben keeps going with his awful rhymes until I'm up and out of bed.

"Ben," I say, "don't try to rhyme, you moldy lime." I like words a lot, and I'm good at rhyming them. I'm much better at rhyming than my brother, Ben, in my opinion, and I have *lots* of opinions.

"Dolores!" Ben shouts again. He knows I don't like being called that—I like my nickname Lola much better. My middle name is Esther and I like that. According to Grandma Levine, my *bubbe*, Esther means "star" in Hebrew.

"Wanna hear a joke, Lola?" Ben asks. He likes telling jokes. "What do kitties eat for dessert?"

"I don't know," I grumble.

"*Mice* cream!" he says. "Get it? Get it? 'Mice' instead of 'ice.'"

"I get it," I say. Ever since Mom and Dad agreed that we could get a kitty this summer, Ben's started with the cat jokes.

I stretch my hands toward the ceiling. If I jump up, I can almost touch the stars Dad and I painted on the ceiling a few weeks ago. It was really fun—until I got paint in my eyes. After that, Mom made

sure both Dad and I wore goggles when we decided to paint ceilings. Ben thought our paint goggles looked cool, so now he wears them even when he isn't painting. They're big and round, and I think they make him look like a bug.

Now Ben's trying to touch his hands to the ceiling, too, only he thinks it will be easier if he jumps off my dresser.

Thwunk! He lands on the floor, hard. *Thwunk! Kerplunk!* He tries again.

This time Dad yells. "What's going on up there? Hurry or you'll be late for school!" He and Mom take turns driving us to school each morning.

Mom must have an early assignment for the newspaper, because she's gone by the time we get downstairs. Dad's making pancakes, but it's taking really long because he is trying to make them into different shapes. Dad's an artist who believes in creative expression—even with pancakes. Sometimes, when I am upset, he gives me a piece of paper and a pencil and tells me to draw my feelings. I like art, but I like words better than pictures when it comes to feelings. Finally, the pancakes are ready.

"Mine looks like an ear," Ben complains.

"It's a whale," Dad says. "See the blueberry eye?"

"I thought that was an earring," Ben says.

I'm not sure what my pancake is, but I don't want to hurt Dad's feelings, so I say,

"Looks great, Dad," and bite into what I think is a snail. I think Dad's better with paint.

In the driveway, we get into Dad's orange car—what Dad calls his people mover. I guess the people mover doesn't move very fast, because it takes forever to warm up and we are late for school. I get sent to the office for a late slip.

"Hi, Principal Blot!" I say, peeking into her office. Principal Blot isn't just my principal. She's also the mother of my super best friend, Josh Blot. She looks up from her desk.

"Good morning, Lola," she says with a frown. Principal Blot frowns a lot, especially around me.

"Are you in trouble?" she asks.

"No!" I say. "I'm just late. It's because my dad was making creative pancakes, and our people mover was slow." Principal Blot looks up at the ceiling and takes a deep breath. Her ceiling is plain white.

"I've got stars on my ceiling, Principal Blot. You should come over and see them—"

"Lola!" Principal Blot interrupts. "Aren't you late for class?"

"Yes," I say.

"So, shouldn't you get going?" she asks.

"Yes!" I say, and start to sprint to class. But I have my backpack on, and I guess I forgot to zip it, because everything spills out.

"Lola! No running in the halls," Principal Blot says. "You know better than that."

"Sorry, Principal Blot. I forgot. I hope you're not exasperated, Principal Blot." My mom uses the word "exasperated" a lot. She says it is a nice way of saying that you're annoyed. It's a cool word, in my opinion.

"Lola," Principal Blot says. "If you don't get going right now, I promise I *will* be exasperated. Now walk, *don't run*, to class."

Be seen with Lola Levine!

Catch all of Lola's
wild adventures
in the second grade!